THE
CLINTON
MAFIA

THE CLINTON MAFIA

VONDA CROCKER

CITIOFBOOKS, INC.
3736 Eubank NE Suite A1
Albuquerque, NM 87111-3579
www.citiofbooks.com
Hotline: 1 (877) 389-2759
Fax: 1 (505) 930-7244

Ordering Information:

Quantity sales. Special discounts are available on quantity purchases by corporations, associations, and others. For details, contact the publisher at the address above.

Printed in the United States of America.

ISBN-13:   Paperback   979-8-89391-733-8
                  eBook   979-8-89391-735-2
                  Hardback   979-8-89391-734-5

Library of Congress Control Number: 2025911491

Table Of Contents

Chapter One

The road curved through the tiny town of Vulture Creek then gently rose up Vulture Mountain. Everyone hated the name but never got around to changing it. At the top of the last rise, one could get a glimpse of Lake Duberry sparkling in the far valley. At night in the valley below, the town of Clinton's light caused a glow in the night sky. Cruise control at 60 allowed a fast but safe decent through moderate curves to the mountain base. Various businesses began to appear. the Methodist College spread out on the right with the Clinton General Hospital on the left.

In summer months local farmers pulled their pickups under the huge oaks to sell their produce. Walmart across the street didn't deter their business.

As the county seat, the county courthouse sat in the middle of an aging square.

Old timers remembered before the by-pass when the road curved through town. In those days the Baxter Hotel was busy but now sat in dismal disrepair.

The for-sale sign was faded and hanging by one rusty nail. Fortunately, it was a block off the square.

On the square, Tony's Appliance Store handled the standard good brands. Unlike some big chains, Tony would take your old appliance away for free after installing the new one.

The coffee shop "The Brewery" did a good business as did "Sweet Elegance" the local dress shop and tearoom.

One the next street around the courthouse Tiffany Ann Beaudreau Investments was flanked by Clinton Chamber of Commerce and R. J. Murphy's Surprise Gift Shop.

On the next street one would find Loudersmith, Attorney at Law, and Valita's Flower Shoppe and the Clinton Police Station. Three beauty shops were crowded in between other businesses.

Efforts to dress up the square had baskets of flowers hanging from the new streetlights. Repurposed chimney flues served as flowerpots and placed on either side of the benches on the sidewalks. A two-block stretch of sidewalk had been replaced with brick paving. Cleverly decorated bicycles painted by local artist were permanently parked on street corners. It was a small southern town valiantly trying to stay alive.

Chapter Two

Lavern and Floyd Jones were once again, on a two-week pleasure trip.

They loved visiting out of the way places, wandering around tiny towns and camping in their Coleman Camper at local camp sites. They picked Clinton because it was halfway to the final destination they had mapped out.

They found the campsite at Lake Duberry with no trouble. After unhooking the camper, and setting up camp they were too tired to wander into town for a meal.

Sitting at the picnic table they discussed how relaxing it was to be in such a quiet area where really nothing exciting ever happens.

Chapter Three

On that same cloudless evening, Emmett Smith aka Lorenzo Martinez was coming down the last stretch of Vulture Mountain into town.

He was six feet of muscle with a small pouch which was getting bigger every year because of the tequila he loved. His head was shaved with a tattoo above the right ear of a marijuana leaf inside a heart.

He had grown up dirt poor but with a burning desire not to be. He had a reputation for taking any job that paid well with no questions asked. He was rarely unemployed.

There was not one ounce of compassion or kindness in his makeup. No one still living remembered him ever smiling.

Emmet absolutely hated this job. Every week he had to make the insufferably boring drive from Mobile Alabama to this tiny town of Clinton to pick up five pounds of stupid fudge from that frumpy little Consuela Lopez. She was a scared little rabbit, and she should be, he thought. Her little family back home could disappear with one phone call. It was so easy to control those illegally or even legally in the states just as long as they had family in the old country.

When he was offered this job, it seemed too easy for the money, but he hadn't counted on how boring it was going to be.

He was letting his non-descript Ford Bronco set its own speed as he leaned down to adjust his radio and plug in his phone to recharge. The last thing he saw when he finally looked up was the rear of the loaded gravel truck pulling out in from of him.

The local paper covered the tragedy briefly but since the local police were having trouble contacting next of kin the name of the deceased was not published. Also not to mention was the two kilos of cocaine found in a side panel of the vehicle. They also never mentioned they would never have found it if the crash hadn't triggered the super secured panel to pop open.

As in every town the wreck was soon old news.

The drugs were locked up securely, Emmett was on ice at the local mortuary and life went on.

However, his death was about to cause waves across several southern states as the local sheriff filed it away.

Chapter Four

It was only eight p.m. on that starlit night and the town square appeared deserted.

Sweet Elegance was completely dark with one exception. A tiny sliver of light could be seen under a closed door in the far corner of the dress shop and tearoom.

Behind the closed door, Savanna Sue Morgan sat in front of her cluttered desk surrounded by ledgers piled three deep.

Her usually perfectly coiffed hair was tousled from her nervous fingers running through it and a frown marred her usually serene features.

She sat back with a sigh, reached for the cup of cold tea, sipping as she stretched her cramped legs.

For two months now she had felt something was amiss. Her marriage seemed solid. Her children appeared happy and her grandchild was perfect so what was it?

The constant flow of customers, most of whom bought something, had her ending the day with a smile.

Tonight, she had decided to go back a few months in the ledgers.

Somehow the constant stream of customers wasn't coinciding with her end of month inventory tally. She had checked and rechecked, but all the numbers appeared correct. They just didn't match the inventory. Every dress shop owner expected shop lifting but that had never been a problem in their little town.

There was only a bit over two thousand living in Clinton, but summer brought hundreds of tourists to the nearby lake. Hundreds more stopped by enroute to bigger venues north.

The tearoom had experienced phenomenal sales of Savanna's homemade fudge, especially the dark chocolate. She supposed the slack economy at least let people buy sweets. All the numbers from the tearoom matched the ledgers.

She brought each of her staff to mind examining each with a critical eye.

Marvis Thompsom and Iris Poindexter, both in their eighties, had been delighted to work two days a week, giving Savanna a much-needed day off. They had been helping out for ten years with never a hint of misconduct. Mentally erasing their names, she continued with her list.

Bobby Sue Beaudrou worked the tearoom and the dress shop on weekends when it was especially busy. Savanna was great friends with her mother Tiffiany Ann. With a deep sigh she mentally put her under the watch column.

Savannas own daughter Missy Leigh helped in the shop most days but she too had felt something amiss. The cleaning lady Consuela Lopez was a darling short plump lady who came in and out like a whirlwind. After she left, the shop smelled especially clean. She had recently learned to make the fudge on Saturdays which gave Savanna Sue even more free time. Consuela's name went in the watch column.

Where in the world was the discrepancy? She couldn't settle down and couldn't figure it out so she abruptly stood up slamming the last ledger closed. She gathered her jacket and purse locked the office door and headed out the front door. She was so distraught she almost left the front door unlocked but habit had her turning back to secure the door.

The girls were meeting tonight for wine, and she desperately wanted that glass of wine. They would have snacks in lieu of dinner. Perhaps they could help her figure it out.

Chapter Five

Valita Faye Adair was expecting the girls for wine and snacks. It was always a perfect break in routine for them all.

Valita was a tall buxom blond who had grown up in Clinton. Her daddy Bubba Bradford had served as town mayor as had her granddaddy before him. The Bradfords also were a prodigious family so one never knew who was related to whom. It helped keep the gossip to the minimum.

In high school, Valita had fallen head over heels in love with Mark Adair the star quarterback for the Clinton Falcons. It wasn't a surprise they married right out of high school. Mark had worked as a city police officer then on to the state police academy where he excelled. He was eventually assigned to the Clinton area, so they were essentially back home. Everyone said he knew everything that happened in the area.

They had no children so Valita, who absolutely loved plants and getting her hands dirty, opened the town's only flower shop, Valita's Flower Shoppe. Her elegant exterior hid a fun spirit that erupted when least expected. Once after several glasses of wine, she disclosed that years earlier she had gotten tipsy and danced on the bar at Coyote Ugly.

Valita bustled about the kitchen setting out a few snacks, opening two bottles of wine to breath and finally wiping crumbs off her ample chest. The girls would arrive any minute and she just couldn't wait.

The past week in her flower shop had been long and stressful. There had been a wedding and three funerals, so she needed this respite.

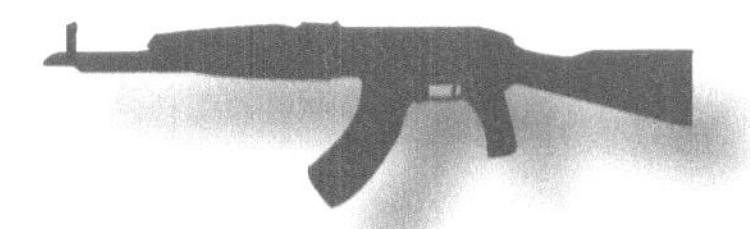

Chapter Six

The first to arrive was Rozalyn Murphy who was called Roz by her friends. She had graduated from Clinton High School and then from the State University with a business degree. She returned to Clinton to care for her mother who had been diagnosed with Alzheimer's disease.

Roz had moved into the family home on the hill above town. After a year of constant care of her mother, she was suddenly left alone, when her mother died of a heart attack.

Roz spent a month clearing all the paperwork associated with the death. She was amazed at the amount of money her mother had squirreled away, as she inherited the money and the house. She was at loose ends as to what to do next.

One evening she looked around the two-story house at all the beautiful nick knacks her mother had collected on her many trips abroad after Roz's dad had passed away. The idea of a gift shop grew quickly into a reality.

Roz named it Surprise as the money to start it had been a surprise.

She bought an old storefront on the square, spent a month gutting and renovating, doing much of the work herself.

Surprise opened with a grand opening serving champagne and elegant hor d'oeuves.

Just to look around the town, one would assume there was little surplus money but the money was there. As in many southern towns the real money was not something one flaunted. One just had it.

Surprise was a huge success. Roz used her dear friends as an idea cache for new items online. Her spiky hair cut was so blond it appeared white and her designer jeans and crisp white shirts were known all over town. She was often hailed when seen only from the rear.

Roz was greeted with a huge hug and squeals.

Right behind Roz, Tammy Logan walked up.

Tammy owned half of Clinton. She had quietly bought up large parcels at land sales and bankruptcy thinking she had rather put money in land than the stock market.

Her late husband didn't like to travel so she was making up for lost time managing at least one big trip a year. The money Bobby Ray, rest his soul, had so carefully tucked away, allowed Tammy to do as she wished. Somedays she even threw out McDonald containers instead of washing and reusing as Bobby Ray had insisted, she do. That gave her a real sense of power.

Her second husband married her because her first had been so successful. Tammy divorced him within a year. The sex just wasn't worth it!

Although she had grown up in another state, she met her first husband while visiting an aunt in Clinton.

She was a beautiful woman with a gorgeous complexion, coal black curly hair and deep green eyes. She rarely wore makeup and caused people to take a second look. She never seemed to notice, her friends kept her grounded and at peace.

Chapter Seven

As the girls poured wine, they heard the door open, and Savanna sailed in. Savanna Sue was a true southern beauty. At 5'5" she kept her figure rigorously under control. Her thick dark hair brushed her shoulders, and her complexion was movie star perfect. At fifty-five years old Savanna had the perfect skin of a woman half her age. She swore her secret was never sunbathing a day in her life.

She married her high school sweetheart Ted Morgan. Ted was the high school basketball coach so during basketball season they could always be found at games. They had three children, Missy Leigh who married Jordan Jones a banker. Missy Leigh helped Savanna Sue at the dress shop.

Brian was a senior at the state university playing basketball and majoring in business. Jules was a senior in high school and much to his father's dismay he played the tuba in the band. He had NO interest in sports. As she entered the kitchen, she said one word – "WINE"!

Next through the door was Constance Buffington Hightower who was affectionately called Buffy. Her late husband Tom was an editor of a state newspaper. She was widowed when he died in a freak car accident shortly after their tenth anniversary. She drives several days a week around the state eating at interesting restaurants to find fodder for her column "Nosh Notes" that appears weekly in the state paper. Thus, she is always on a diet!

At 5'5" she hovers between 135 pounds and 195. Her seesaw diets would have made another popular column. Her girlfriends assured her, if she was a rail, no one would believe her Nosh Notes. A food critic is expected to carry some extra weight. Buffy ended up in Clinton, after her husband died, by throwing a dart at the state map. She felt she had to start fresh in a new place. She brought a small house in town. It had a miniscule yard she could mow with a push mower and nice enough neighbors. She was absent a lot traveling around the state and writing up her notes. The one thing she truly enjoyed about her new town was the group of wonderful friends she had made.

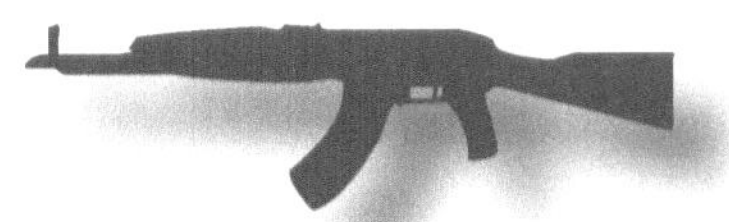

Chapter Eight

Coming in behind Buffy was Beatrice Lowell Lauderside affectionately called Bella. She had graduated from Harvard Law subsequently passing the bar in three states before she met her husband Carlos Manchetti in New York. After only two years of wedded bliss Carlos was gunned down in a bistro off Time Square. She really knew so little of Carlos's background but not being stupid she could add two and two!

Her aunt Sue Lauderside died about the same time leaving Bella her money and a house in Clinton. Belle immediately packed up, sold the apartment in New York, leaving no forwarding address and moved south to Clinton. She reverted to her maiden name, passed the state bar with flying colors, hung out her shingle, and ten years later she was even speaking with a slight southern accent.

Belle was what southerners call a "big girl". She was 5'11"and weighed over 200 lbs. She never dieted, loved a good meal and was addicted to Hot Tamale Candy. There was always a bag near her. Her mane of light brown hair hung to her shoulders from a sever center part. Her deep blue eyes could look straight through you. She was universally feared in the court room. The local restaurants loved to see her come as she ate out at least one meal a day. Not only that, but she also never asked for a doggy bag because there were never any leftovers. It was a joy for the chefs to watch her enjoy their presentations. She also had a big heart for helping others, often taking odd things in lieu of attorney fees.

The last to arrive was Tiffany Ann Beaudreau. Tiffy was the only daughter of the New Orleans Beaudreau's. She was on so many boards she needed an I Pad to keep up. Her spiked brown hair, streaked with blond was worn in a pixie.

She opened her own investment firm immediately after graduating summa cum laud from L.S.U. She adored her pharmacist husband Phillip for taking her out of New Orleans and out from under the suffocating devotion of her doting parents. She loved them dearly but was no longer ten years old. They visited often, always lamenting that Tiffany was stuck in this hick town. Tiffany loved living in the close-knit town and truly loved her close friends. Her husband had graduated from L.S.U. but grew up in Clinton where he opened his pharmacy and neither wanted to be anywhere else.

Tiffany and Phillip had one daughter, Bobbie Sue. Tiffany was determined not to suffocate her as she herself had been growing up. They gave her a great deal of freedom to be all she could be. Often this caused sleepless nights worrying they had been too lax. So far Bobbie Sue had not been arrested so thus far, all was well. She even worked part-time in Savanna's dress shop.

Her investment firm was very successful as she had made a great deal of money for a lot of people. Word of her expertise spread so now she could pick and choose clients. They built a large home on the nearby lake where they entertained monthly. Her favorite escape was a regular gathering of her dearest Clinton friends.

Chapter Nine

As the door closed behind the last girlfriend; the noise level rose accordingly. The group of friends had bonded instantly during a fund raiser for the library some years before. On a lovely winter evening the good friends decided to attend a locally produced play at the country club. Rarely did they get a chance to really dress up, so they dressed to the nines, including full length mink coats. They had gathered beforehand for a glass of wine before piling into one SUV for the trip to the venue.

On the way to the county club, Belle called to make sure of the time. She was stunned to hear the venue had changed. The play would now take place at the nearby local Veterans of Foreign War (VFW). By this time, they were running late. Finally arriving, they hustled into the large room. They threw their furs over the stack of metal folding chairs and here horrified someone had saved them a table in the middle of the room. Everyone in the audience had gotten the change of venue earlier and were in sweatshirts and blue jeans.

Someone yelled, loud enough to be heard in the next county, "Oh my god! it's the Clinton Mafia". The name stuck and the group was forever branded; it was amazing to each of the group that they were such a close group since they were so different. The true sisterly love they had for each other was unflappable. If one faced a difficulty, they all did their best to help.

Chapter Ten

Everyone had found a spot around the large kitchen table and were catching each other up on events since the last time they gathered. Belle was very observant due to her many years as an attorney; she was feared by her court opponents. For one thing she could spot a lie, fabrication or a loophole by watching the eyers and body language. Looking around the table, she brought those clever eyes back to Savannah Sue. What gives? She queried. All eyes swiveled to Savanna. "Oh, it's probably nothing "Savanna protested. "Really!"

"Maybe not; but you know you can share anything with us. Maybe we can help." The other women quieted uneasily since thy hadn't noticed Savannah's disquiet. "Oh, it really is probably nothing, "Savannah repeated. After a pause she continued, "it's just that my books don't line up with inventory, but I can't figure out why. It should be a simple numbers problem, but it isn't. Besides that, we are selling a hell of a lot of fudge, excuse my French and I'm not complaining, mind you, but I do find it a bit odd."

Your fudge is especially good" RJ interjected "the word of how good just got around. If you want a fabulous fudge, go to Sweet Elegance! As to the inventory, do you have security cameras? Shoplifting is a big problem in my store, but the obvious security cameras cut it back to next to nothing."

"My cameras are fake and anyway, I can't use them in the dressing rooms. Maybe I should get real ones for the rest of the shop." "If you do," Belle suggested, "I'd not tell anyone, even your most trusted employees." Savannah Sue looks stunned, "Y'all don't think any of my employees could be responsible!" musing she continued slowly, "although I did mentally make a list earlier and thought maybe I should watch a couple of them in the future. It made me sick to do even that". Tammy Faye put her glass down with undue force saying, "Girls let's all keep our eyes and ears open an solve this mystery." Laughing Roz said, "Oh no! the Clinton Mafia rides again!"

As the wine and snacks were consumed and some made motions to depart the conversation returned to Savannah's problem. Tiff touched Savannah's arm. "Do you want me to take a look? Sometimes another set of eyes can see something new." Oh, Tiffany Ann, would you? I would be so grateful. I've looked at them so much, nothing seems right." "Of course," Tiff replied, "How about tomorrow after work for both of us." In a very quiet voice, she added "If you want, I'll ask my security company to send a man over after hours to install real cameras." With a sigh of relief, Savannah nodded her eager agreement. "Remember now," reminded Tiff, "don't tell a soul the cameras will be real, not even Missy Leigh!" The evening came to a reluctant end as hugs were shared, goodbye called and drive safe echoed through the door.

Chapter Eleven

Savannah Sue opened the door for Tiffany Ann and an attractive young man in nondescript jeans and jean jacket. "I brought Jason Taggett incognito to install your cameras" Tiff explained as the door shut them in. "I didn't think you would want anyone seeing a man with security logo all over his clothes. Jason is the best and after tonight he will forget he has been here." "Are you sure we need all this cloak and dagger?' asked Savannah. Tiff replied "Precaution never hurt!"

Jason spent two hours installing the new surveillance system. He connected them to a password protected site on Savannah's computer. She could check the surveillance anytime she wanted. It was motion triggered as in the dead of night it wouldn't film a dark empty room. Jason suggested she check the feed every evening when she was alone in her office. Savannah thanked him profusely, and hugged Tiffany tightly saying, "Thanks, you're the best!!

For a week Savannah Sue religiously checked the camera feed with nothing recorded out of the ordinary. She watched customers come and go. Some disappeared into the dressing room to try on clothes, but they appeared to bring out what the took into the room. The tearoom was alternately crowded then deserted. Every Saturday she noted Consuella making a large box of fudge. How odd she thought. She asked her daughter to help keep an eye on things explaining that something was amiss. "Please don't say a word to anyone or hurt feelings unnecessarily." Looking worried, Missy promised, and she thought she would be more vigilant while she was in the shop. She tried to think back if anything or anyone seemed off. Shaking her head, she put it on the back burner to worry about later.

Chapter Twelve

Tiffany was worried about Savanna Sue but encouraging her to put in security and going over her books was about all she knew to do. She had given the books a quick look the night before. She too had found nothing. There was something amiss but without cross checking everything it would be impossible to tell exactly what.

When they moved to Clinton for Phillip to open his pharmacy and she moved her investment firm. She was gratified so many of her clients followed her. She was THAT good. It was also giving an added benefit to escape the suffocating demands of being an Beaudreau with multiple family members thinking she would welcome their advice.

To be a member of the Clinton Mafia gave her just the undemanding support group like she had always dreamed. She still had girl friends in New Orleans but her friends here were the dearest. They also didn't give a fig she was a Beaudreau.

Tiff and Phillip always went to a yearly pharmacy conference where new drugs were discussed as well as new information on laws etc. This year the conference was in Mobile, Alabama. They always made the conference a long weekend and she was really looking forward to this break. She put Savannah Sue's worries on the back burner to think more about when they returned.

They left on Friday. Phillip had made reservation at the Mobile hotel to be ready for the next early meeting Saturday morning. Phillip suggested they have dinner at a new Mexican restaurant within walking distance of the hotel. After freshening up a bit, they walked arm in arm down the street.

As they waited on a table Tiff excused herself to go to the lady's room. No one was in the room, so she slipped into the last stall and was on the verge of relieving herself when the main door burst open and she heard angry male voices. She first thought she was in the wrong bathroom so she pulled her feet up and tried hard not to pee. Her Spanish kicked in and she interpreted the first harsh voice. "Shut up you idiot someone may be in here!" A more frightened voice loudly whispered, "I don't see anyone and didn't see anyone come in before us. And don't tell me to shut up. If you had told Juan the fudge was delivered on time, we wouldn't be in this mess. Why didn't you meet Emmit like always?" The first voice hissed, "He didn't show! We will be on the hook for it, so you better be heading north to see what going on. Now, get out of here before some lady comes in. I'll meet you at the usual place next Sunday and you better know something. Get lost!" Tiff slowly let out her breath, not even realizing she had been holding it. She heard the door open and a female voice saying "Opps! This is the ladies' room, right?" A stall door opened and when she heard someone relieving themselves, she followed suit. She flushed when the other toilet flushed. Peeking through the door crack, she watched as the woman washed and dried her hands then departed. At least it was the right bathroom! In case the owners of the male voices were watching, she waited until another two ladies came in before she washed her hands and left. "What took you so long?" Phillip demanded. "Oh, just a little problem with the stall door," Tiff replied. If Phillip noticed she was reflectively quiet during dinner he didn't comment.

Tiff absolutely couldn't wait to get back to Clinton and the mafia. On the way out of town they made a quick stop in Fairhope so Tiff could dash into Cat's Meow to purchase a few gifts. When they returned to Clinton, Tiffany was so busy she totally forgot the bathroom incident.

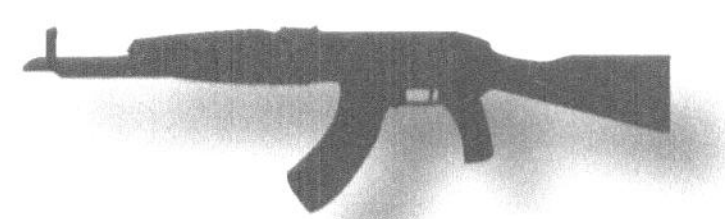

Chapter Thirteen

Tiffany Ann kept thinking of Savannah's problem with the books, so she closed the ledgers she had been perusing and called her "Are you busy?" she asked when Tiff answered, "No more than usual, what's up?" I was just thinking of your books and wanted to offer another set of eyes. "What are you doing after closing the shop?" Tiffany replied, "Ted has a basketball game, but I can miss one. Come on over when we close. You can check out the new Southern Lady. Just in case anyone asks, and you need an excuse."

At six o'clock, after closing her office, Tiffany walked around the square to Sweet Elegance. Savannah Sue was watching for her and unlocked the door. Tiff was yanked inside to a smothering hug "I can't thank you enough!!" Savannah gushed. Tiff patted her on the back and said, "What are friends for, if not to help each other? Now, let's really look at those ledgers." At ten o'clock, Tiff signed deeply and said, "Darling, you have a very clever thief working for you!" What? Who? How? Savannah Sue sputtered. "Very cleverly!" Tiff answered. Let's start with who. One of your elderly helpers. I think it is probably Iris Pointdexter." "But that simply not possible!" Savannah sputtered. "She has been with me 10 years!" "Nevertheless, Savannah, that is what the facts present." "What? How?" Savannah asked and "When"? Well, from what I can gather, and it was well hidden, every week for several months from one to three expensive items were taken with tags switched or destroyed. One might even caulk it up to routine shop lifting. But it's the consistency and the value as well as the size that belies that theory. Also, the discrepancy happens the days Iris worked. Savannah Sue slumped into her chair shaking her head. "Tiff, I made a list of all those who worked here and those two never made the maybe list! How do I handle this??"

Tiffany replied, "First you watch the cameras for those days Iris works, and you watch carefully. She doesn't know they are real, does she? "Oh no, of course not!! No one does!" Tiff continued" Excellent! You can call the law or since this is so foreign to who she has been all these years, you may want to privately confront her and hear what she has to say. You know she has to have a good reason. She may be reselling items on eBay or some other better reason. You can't really decide till you know the why of it. "Yes, yes you are quite right," Savannah sighed. 'I'll do as you advise. Wait, watch and privately confront. It just breaks my heart! Thank you, dear friend, for your time and expertise." "No biggy Tiff. Now did you say you have some new Southern Lady merchandise?? Getting first dibs, that's my fee!" Laughing, they both left the tiny office and headed to the clothing side of Sweet Elegance.

Chapter Fourteen

A week later with the closed sign on the door, Savannah Sue sat in her tiny office searching the camera feeds as they recorded the activities of their clients and the help. She watched as during a lull, with no one in the store, Iris Poindexter selected an expensive pair of slacks, carefully folded them into a plain gift box, removed all tags which she slipped into her bra and wrapped the box in plain white paper. Pulling a large bow from her bag, she taped it to the center of the box. She then carefully tucked the box into her large handbag then turning cheerfully greeted a customer who had just walked in the door. Stunned to see Iris in action, Savannah Sue put her head in her arms and sobbed.

The next morning, she asked Iris to come in for an hour or so to cover. Iris immediately agreed but when she appeared she was a bit surprise to see Mavis Thompson there as well. Savannah Sue met Iris at the door and taking her arm gently said," Iris dear, come on back to the office for a minute." When they got into the tiny office, Savannah closed the door offering the second chair to Iris. Savannah sat in from of the desk but turned to Iris, patted her hand which was tightly gripping the chair arm and calmly asked "Why did you steal from me, Iris? Was it money you needed? Why steal clothes from my store? I give you a discount!" Great hacking sobs shock Iris as she put her head in her hands and began to rock. "I just want to understand, Iris! Why now after ten years of trust?" Savannah waited patiently until the sobs subsided to hiccups. Then in a watery voice Iris said, "Lillian." Stunned, Savannah repeated, "Lillian, your granddaughter, Iris! Why?" In a choked voice Iris said, "When Lillian was small, I could get her fun things at the Dollar Store, and she loved them. But the older she got, her other grandparents gave her more and more expensive gifts, you know like iPad, cell phone, trips! I can't afford any of those things. I don't want her to think I love her less, then they do, but I just don't have the money to compete. The first time I took something and gave it to her, she was deliriously happy. It just got to be a habit to win the gift game occasionally. I'm so ashamed and very sorry Savannah Sue. I know you will fire me and call the sheriff." Iris, you know in your heart of hearts that you can't buy her love. She would be horrified to know you think so little of her. She is not too young to know that you can't afford those gifts. You can show your love for her in a thousand other ways. Free ways!"

"How?" Iris asked tearfully. "Well, first off, don't you go on a camping and hiking weekend every fall? I know you do, so take her with you! Her other grandparents would die rather than spend a night in a tent! Share your life with her with unconditional love. Those are gifts you can give." Iris lifted tear drenched eyes to Savannah Sue". You're going to fire me, aren't you?" "What? Do you think I should? "Fire me and good riddance! I will pay you back Savannah, but it will take a while." "Well don't rob a bank to do it! Let's do this. You will continue here as you have been minus the thieving at half salary until I'm in paid back. Grandparenting can be hard!" Iris let out a huge sigh. "Oh, yes!" Half salary it is. Now I'll have to live to be a hundred! Thank you, Savannah Sue. Thank you from the bottom of my heart!"

When the door closed behind Iris, Savannah called Tiffany Ann. When Tiff picked up, Savannah said, "you were right! Iris just left and you won't believe the reason!! After rehashing the conversation she had with Iris, Tiffany replied, "Savannah Sue, you old softie, but you handled it perfectly. Handled any other way she would have been destroyed in this town and her granddaughter would have lost all respect for her. This is a win/win! Ya done good, girlfriend. Oh! And Savannah, I think we can just tell everyone else, there is a glitch in the books so mystery solved. The security needs to stay with no one knowing it is not the old fake."

Chapter Fifteen

Consuela Lopez was at home in her tiny apartment she rented just off the square. She had a list of businesses she cleaned most days during the week and on Saturday, she cleaned and then made batches of fudge for Sweet Elegance. That last job was what had her pacing her tiny living room/dining room combo. She had just gotten home from Sweet Elegance and had been stunned to find the last 5 pounds of special dark chocolate fudge was still there! The big man with mean eyes and bald head had not picked it up. What did it mean and what was she to do? She thought of calling home in Mexico but terrified of what she would discover. Her sweet babies were with her parents and she had to keep them safe. What to do? What to do?

She had prepared to make the new batch but without the big man's special enclosure she didn't see the need. She always marked it "Special Order". To assure no one else got it. As she paced her tiny floor, miles to the south and even scarier man was heading her way to get answers. Sunday night at midnight he coasted down the final decline into Clinton. He passed over the spot in the highway his cohort had bought it. It was too late to reconnoiter so he checked into Motel 8 as Bill Smith. The next morning after breakfast at McDonalds he walked around the square, just happening to step into Sweet Elegance. "Oh fudge!" he gushed! Savannah Sue walked over to help him. "What kinds do you have? He queried". Savannah rattled off the list. He listed alternatively then said I just love dark chocolate fudge and it appears there's a box over there. "Oh, sorry, sighed Savannah, that's a special order that wasn't picked up. I couldn't sell it. "Freshness doesn't matter to me. I just love fudge. I'll buy it and take if off your hands". Savannah: looked confused but as it was getting old, she sold it to him a half price. He left thinking now easy that had been.

The next day he returned saying how delicious it was and wondering if she made it. "No, Consuela Lopez makes it on Saturday she told him but began to wonder about the entire conversation. It was the first time anyone had asked who made it.

It was easy for him to find Consuela with a few general questions at the Mexican restaurant and the gas station. When he knocked on her door that night, she fearfully let him in. She stood wringing her hands as he sprawled on her little sofa. "What happened on Saturday, Consuela?" "Sir, I do not know! He never came!!! I put it on shelf with sign in case he came later but when I got in this Saturday it was still there! I didn't know what to do." "Did you tell anyone?" he asked quietly. "No, No Senor, I did NOT!' "Okay", he said. "This is what you will do. You will go in Saturday as planned and make a new 5-pound batch for me with this special wrapped special ingredient in it like before. You understand what will happen to your family in Mexico, if you do not. Si?" "Oh, Si,Si Senor. I will do as you ask, please do not hurt my family.," She begged. "As long as you obey me, they will remain safe. Little Maria is SO adorable." As he let himself out the door, he heard her muffled sobs and smiled. Climbing in his car, he headed toward Kansas City with the fudge.

Chapter Sixteen

Rozelyn Murphy sent emails to the mafia asking for help. She had made lasagna and needed them to help her eat it. Everyone replied on they would be there with wine, salad, bread, and dessert. Perfect was the reply. As the gathered with the obligatory hug, air kisses and moans over the aroma from Roz's kitchen they spread out their dishes on the counter. The plates and silver were already on the table. Tammy Faye cooed "Are these dishes from your shop? May I copycat? I love them!" "They are, you may and I'm so glad you love them" RJ replied. As the girls filled their plates, poured wine and found a seat at the kitchen table, RJ asked, "Hey, Savannah did you ever figure out what was wrong with your books?" "Oh yeah". The others echoed. "Well as it turns out it was a simple mistake I found with Tiffs help. No biggy. But the weirdest thing! Remember the volume of fudge sales I told you about?" Everyone nodded with mouths full.

"Well, last week a stranger came in asking for fudge. Gushing really which was strange as it sounded fake as all get out. And frankly he didn't look like a natural gusher! Not only that but he bought that five-pound box of special-order fudge that had been unclaimed for days! I sold it to him for half price. Another thing, when Consuela saw it was still there, she nearly fainted. It was very odd. Then she didn't seem surprised it was gone. Now the last Saturday she made another five-pound box of for the gushy guy who returned and bought it. Nobody normal buys five pounds of fudge week after week. I love the sales but it's just bizarre!"

"Oh, my land!!!", Tiffany screamed. Everyone jumped, sloshing wine right and left. "What the heck, Tiff?" Tammy cried. "Oh, sorry!" Tiff apologized. I just now remembered and it may be part of this fudge mystery.

Remember when Phillip and I went to Mobile for the conference? I totally forgot this, and it is exciting." What". They all asked as one "Well, I was in the restaurant's ladies' room when two men – yes men- stepped into the bathroom yelling at each other. I pulled by feet up so they would think they were alone and honestly wondered if I had inadvertently gone into the wrong restroom. My Spanish is pretty darn good, and they were talking about a shipment that didn't arrive. One of them told the other one to go north and find out what happened to the fudge. After they left, I snuck out with some women who had come in afterwards. Then, I forgot all about it! Does it connect do you think? Belle quickly said, "Girls, I know a state trooper who may be able to put these pieces together and since he is married to Valita here, we have an inside tract. I suggest we go that route since our local lawman aren't the sharpest tacks in the box, if you follow me. There was a moment of silence then everyone began talking at once. Valita interrupted, "Ladies, ladies, I have a suggestion. We all have connections in Clinton. Why don't we use them and see if we see this mystery man in any of our stores or hear anyone mentioning him. "Yeah," Buffy, agreed. "Splendid idea, I travel all over the state for Nash Notes so can look out for him. If the comes in next week Savannah, get a picture of him. Tiff and Savannah exchanged a glance. "RJ, he may come in your gift shop. Tammy Faye, you are out and about so you may see him in Walmart or anywhere! Belle interrupted, "We need a license plate as Savannah that's your job but we really must be careful. This doesn't sound very safe to me."

"Belle, call Valita's trooper and see what he says". "What, now? Why not Valita, he's, her husband! Oh, okay. I get it – not a wife calling. I'm on it!" Belle got out her cell phone and called Mark. "Mark, I'm so glad to catch you! The girls and I have a wee bit of a mystery, but it is odd enough that we think you might want to know about it. "This better be good Belle," Mark barked "Cause I'm on surveillance and can't talk long." "It may be nothing, but something is NOT right. When do you get off duty?". "In three hours. I'll call you tomorrow as I have the day off. "Perfect! Thanks." "Okay girls let's get this down on paper, so I don't make a mess of it. "Tammy why don't you meet him with Valita and me at Valita's in the morning. Will that work?" "Absolutely," they chorused.

Chapter Seventeen

The next morning at Valita's, Mark met Belle, Tammy and Valita in their living room. "What's up ladies and Darling?' "We have a bit of a mystery. First, every Saturday for months Consuela Lopez makes a lot of fudge and has a standing special order for five pounds. Several Saturdays ago, the "steely eyed" man Savannah says buys it didn't show, and Consuela appeared scared. Then a few days later another strange man pops into Sweet Elegance and buys the old fudge – all five pounds. Then this past Saturday he comes in again for another five pounds of special order. Nobody eats that much fudge in a week! Weirdest of all was what Tiffancy Ann heard in Mobile. After repeating Tiff's bathroom story, the girls all stared at Mark. After a moment of stunned silence, Mark gathered himself and said, "So someone buys lot of fudge. So What? A casual conversation overhead miles away. So what?" "Just seems really weird to us". Belle said. "Just remember we told you about it. I think the whole thing smells!" "So noted," Mark sighed, "I'm off to run an errand. See you all soon, I hope."

The minute he was out the door he was on his phone calling his friend who was a Lt. in the Criminal Investigations Division. "Lt Patterson, please when the call went through. "Dave this is Mark, and we need a private meet. I have some new info you and your boys may find interesting." " Well, that was a bust!" Belle sighed. "But I KNOW something isn't right. What's our next step?" Let's gather for lunch and discuss."

At July's Café just off the square, the girls found a table in the corner. Savannah Sue said "Saturday, why don't one of you come by the store and get his license number." "And just how do we do that when we don't know what he drives?" Oh, yeah, small issue." "When he comes in, I'll sneak to the back and call two of you. Y'all either walk down the sidewalk casual like or hide in the courthouse and watch from a window."

"Well, that night work. After we get his license, we should google it. Whoever gets behind his vehicle can have the phone out and surreptitiously take a picture of it,"Buffy suggested. " Yeah, that might work," Valita said, "but y'all this is not some amateur cloak and dagger operation. If this guy is dangerous, we need to be very careful. Who has a camera with a powerful lens?" Belle asked. "I do!" Tammy answered and I think the courthouse is the answer. "Okay, here's what we'll do. When Savannah calls, Tammy and Valita will go casually over to the courthouse and go to the window overlooking Savannah. I think it's the assessor's office, Tammy will take a picture of the license plate and maybe get a shot of him coming out of the door. Valita can make up a story for Savannah Sue. No one will question it," Sounds like a plan, "they agreed. With high fives, the girls divided the bill leaving a generous tip and left going their separate ways.

Chapter Eighteen

In mobile, Alabama Juan Valez aka bill Smith was being questioned about the little snaffle to the north. Juan was assuring his handler that all was well. "The police have no idea about what's going on and I'm positive the fudge deal is still viable. I found out that Lorenzo Martinez is chilling his bones in Clinton's mortuary after a wreck. As far as I could discover they didn't find the cache. The little fudge maker is too terrified for her family to say a word. She is making the fudge just the way we like it. The cocaine is no doubt still in the wrecked Bronco in their compound lot. I can sneak in and retrieve it." "No "snapped the handler. We will write it off and it can get crushed with the Bronco. That way we can swear ignorance should it be found, it has nothing to do with any of us. Do you understand?" "Si! That is probably the smart way to handle it," Juan said sweating profusely. "Tell me Juan," the handler continued, "do you get any vibes in Clinton that people suspect you of anything.?' "No, absolutely not! I know how to blend and have been very clear of my love of fudge. That silly woman was so glad of the sale she smiles every time I come in. It's a little town so anyone coming in to buy is a really good thing. I'm good!" The handler sat back crossed his arms and was silent a moment. "Tell you what Juan, we will make two more runs to Clinton, then we need to move on to another town. Five pounds of fudge is a lot to buy week after week so we will have to move on. Check out if there is another town in the next county, maybe that has a fudge shop. One with a Mexican helping out would be best! Two more weeks Juan. Your little fudge maker needs to understand the consequences to her family should she decide to say anything to anybody!" "Oh, she understands," Juan smirked. " She truly understands!!" "Okay then! Two more runs to Clinton. Leave a day early this time so the town people get used to seeing you on days other than Saturday, you are dismissed,"

As Juan left, his handler pursed his lips, put his fingertips together and sat in thought. It might be a good idea to double check Juan's reliability, calling in his son Rico, he said "Son, I have a small errand for you to run this next weekend." "Sure Dad". Rico replied delighted to be able to get out of town for anything. He might even take his girlfriend to make the drive more enjoyable. A paid night or two in the motel with her would be really sweet and little Angel would be icing on the cake, so to speak. He was grinning like an idiot as he swaggered out the door.

Chapter Nineteen

Mark Adair had scheduled a meeting with Lt. Dave Paterson, his pal in the Criminal Investigation Division, the day after his conversation with the women. He wasn't surprised to find a conference room full of troopers. Captain Morisey was leading the meeting and asked Mark to catch everyone up on what he knew. Mark explained that his wife and her friends seemed to have stumbled on a clever plan to distribute cocaine. He outlined what he knew including the local sheriff finding a kilo of cocaine in the side panel of a demolished Bronco. The driver had been killed but so far not identified.

The Fudge Shop at a local dress shop and a tearoom appeared to be used to hide the cocaine for transporting. The questions were fired rapidly and Mark shared what he knew. Before Captain Morisey could dismiss Mark, he asked to be heard. "Y'all need to know that the women involved on the edge of this are, number one not stupid and number two, won't sit back and wait for y'all to do something. I tried to make it sound silly to even think something is wrong, but these women are called the Clinton Mafia and won't wait long to look at all this more closely." "Is there surveillance at the fudge shop?" One trooper asked. "No, I believe they are fake." "Okay", Captain Morisey said, "I'm setting up a task force for this and we probably need to divide and conquer. Mark, it will look suspicious if more troopers go into Clinton, so we will send in two undercover." "On Saturday one of you will go into the tearoom to get a cup of coffee and hang out about thirty minutes. The others can sit on the Courthouse bench and visit with the other men who always hang out there. Sunglasses if the sun is shining so they can't tell where are looking. You know how to do it!" Mark, are you sure it is just one guy?" "No, not really. It is only one buying fudge but who knows." Okay men, let's get this on paper how we'll snag this fudger." Snickering he left the room. After the meeting Mark went home intending to interrogate his wife.

Chapter Twenty

Saturday began as another beautiful day in Clinton. Savannah Sue raised the blinds on the front picture window showcasing a creative arrangement of accessories to compliment the stunning dress on the manakin. Consuela was humming behind the display shelf of fudge. She had made her usual large batch of dark chocolate fudge wrapping a large box marked "special order." She had already made peanut butter, maple and pistachio. With only blond fudge to go she was feeling calmer. She plugged in the coffee urn and put the electric water kettle on for tea. When the bell tinkled over the door she jumped and slipped behind the storage room door peering through the crack to see who it was. When she realized it was only Missy Leigh she slid back around the door.

Around eleven o'clock a new customer came in and ordered coffee and fudge. At every bell, Consuela ducked out of sight. The man with the coffee slowly drank his coffee and ate his piece of fudge. He appeared to be reading a magazine left on another table.

The bell tinkled again. Consuela ducked out as the large man she recognized as the one who visited her the week before, walked up to the counter and tapped the bell for service. Consuela came out with fear in her eyes. The gentleman asked for his special order. She snatched the heavy box off the shelf, took the payment and nearly fainted. After he paid, he tipped his cap at her and left. The second customer followed him out after a few minutes. Savannah Sue saw him come in so excused herself from her customer to slip into the office and call the girls, "go girls- he's here- cap and big!" she hissed. Tammy had been sitting in the courthouse stairwell adjusting her Nikon. Valita ran up the stairs and they rushed to the window of the assessor's office. "Borrowing your window to take pictures of Sweet Elegance, Miss Mildred," they explained. Miss Mildred lifted a thin hand in okay.

Tammy peered out the window and watched a big man wearing a hat get into a brown SUV she snapped and snapped. As he was driving away, she noticed two more vehicles right behind him. "Hmmmm". She murmured. Valita looked at Tammy with raised eyebrows. Did you recognize any of those cars?' " No mam – did you?" "Nope!"

I don't care what Mark says something is going on around here," Tammy said in a low voice. "I agree," said Valita. Let's go check in with Savannah.

Chapter Twenty-One

As it was Saturday, Savannah Sue closed at 6pm. She closed and locked the door after wishing Consuela a hasty good night, practically shoving her out the door. Turning to each other they all said, "Wine!"

Savannah Sue reach under the cabinet by the front safe retrieving a bottle of PinoGregio. She expertly de-corked the bottle, brought out wine glasses and poured! To the Mafia! Clinking glasses they all sipped.

Under the window in the alley Rico was snuggling with his girlfriend of the moment. If Dad wanted info, he knew how to get it and enjoy himself. Hell!! It sounded like they were stepping in the mafia's territory. This was a bit over their paygrade. He had to get to his phone, PRONTO! He and his lovely Angel slipped quietly out of the alley. Rico practically dragging her to the motel where he was charging his cell phone. He got his dad on the first ring. "Report" his dad commanded. Rico took a deep breath then said "Dad, we are in way over our heads! The women here are associated with the Mafia. One of them had a New York accent she tries to cover-up but I'm too clever to be deceived. The MAFIA, Dad!! What do we do?" "How do you know this, son?". "I was spying on them, and they were drinking wine, toasting to the "Mafia." "This is very concerning son, you come on back now and we will regroup with this new information. In such a small town, too!"

Valita told herself to mind her own business but how to find out who owned the out of state license plate. Her husband was the logical choice. When he finally got home at nine that night, she controlled her desire to pounce on him with her request. Instead, she took a deep breath slid her arms around him, laid her head on his shoulders and cooed "You had a long day, Darling. Want a beer before I heat up dinner?" Expecting the opposite, Mark took a minute to reevaluate the moment. "Sure, sweetheart! What's for dinner? "Tacos, an easy heat up. You just sit down at the table and I'll bring it right after your beer."

Mark frowned as his eyes followed his wife out of the room, and he wondered. Valita poured his beer, sitting it in front of him with a smile. She left and returned a few minutes later with a plate of tacos and refried beans. Sitting down across from him she smiled, "So, how was your day?' "Interesting". He commented between bites. "Tacos are great, Valita. Thanks Babe! I didn't have time to eat today." "Well," she replied, as she slipped a piece of paper over to him. We girls were wondering if you could run that license plate for us. Just for funsies, don't you know."

Mark choked on his last bite of Taco. "Oh, damn it to hell! I knew it!! I just KNEW it!! "Darling, Darling! I told everyone your mafia girls wouldn't let this slide. You just had to investigate by yourselves, didn't you?' "Well, of course!" Valita countered, you said it was nothing, We KNEW it wasn't NOTHING, what is it, Mark?"

"It's big Valita and now you girls are in on the fringe, it scares me for you all! Let's get everyone together in the morning, you girls are going to screw up a big operation if you don't back away." Valita paled, "you could have just thanked us for the info, and you would take care of it."

"We hoped y'all would let it drop". "Well, we didn't! Valita spewed. Mark walked around the table wrapping his arms around her and said, "if anything had happened to you or any of the girls, I would never have forgiven myself." Standing and turning into his arms she said, "The Mafia will meet here tomorrow for coffee. How's That?" "Perfect" he agreed.

Chapter Twenty-Two

After late night phone calls from Valita, each of the Mafia members arrived at Valita's for coffee and fresh cinnamon rolls. "Help yourselves, ladies." After they had eaten, they sat stone faced waiting for Mark to explain. "Okay," he quavered, "here is what I can tell you. There is an organization in Mobile, Alabama that gets pure uncut cocaine. Don't ask because we don't know where it's coming from. It's brought up here and probably lot of other places. Here it is put in a five-pound slab of fudge in sealed bags. Those are purchased and taken to a contact in Kansas City where it is divided to sell in smaller batches."

Belle interrupted, "Why bring cocaine all the way up here to be put in fudge and then sent on to Kansas City? It makes no sense." A very good question, we don't have an answer for yet. We think they are using a group of illegal Mexicans to do their bidding by threatening their families back in Mexico. "Savannah Sue, your Consuela has children back in Mexico and is probably terrified for their safety. I shouldn't be telling any of this but we want you to know how serious this is and you need to step away and let us do our job!"

The girls looked at one another. "Mark, Belle said, "we understand you have stepped over the line for us but please, is there anything we can do to help? We are good at undercover stuff." High fives were given all around. Mark considered for a minute. "It's too bad your store doesn't have real surveillance, Savannah. Sue. We could use some hard evidence." Savannah Sue and Tiffany exchanged glances. Savannah threw up her hands. "Okay, here's the deal! Everything said here stays here. Right?" "Yes, of course" they all agreed. "Okay, after the money problem, which is okay now. I had real cameras put on but no one knows. Not even my own daughter!" She looked around expecting some kick back but only saw understanding and agreement. "Oh, shit! Y'all are the best." She jumped up and hugged each of them

Mark was elated. This tidbit of info was worth the ass kicking he would get for sharing sensitive info with a group of women. "Savannah Sue, you are a treasure! My friend will get in touch to set it up for this this coming Saturday. Also let's keep Consuela doing her thing. She is probably so scared for her family, if she knew she would blab. Are we all agreed here? Low profile and keep on keeping on like you have. We will be putting a bug in Consuela home when she is here! That will keep her and her children safe. When we put all this behind us, she may want to bring them here and apply for citizenship." Savannah said, "She already applied and is just waiting. She has a green card, so she is legal. You don't think this will cause her concern. Her part, I mean." "Na! I think not. Anything else?" Mark asked. All head shook no, so he thanked them for coming and left for work.

For a few minutes after Mark left, the girls just looked at each other, eyes wide and bright. Valita's phone rang; she scrambled back to the counter where she left it. It was Mark. "Listen Darlin, I forgot to tell y'all. There is a young Mexican couple wandering around town that the locals don't know. They may have been sent to snoop and watch the fudge man since the last one died. Y'all keep your eyes open and mouths shut. If you notice them just pay attention where they are and what they are doing. DO NOT play cop!" Valita rang off with a "Thanks, Darlin!" She quickly returned to the Mafia and related the new information. Savannah grinned and said, "Oh I've seen them but thought they must be family visiting one of the Mexican restaurant families. Yahoo, this gives us something to do! The Mafia left quickly and returned to work. Each of them more watchful.

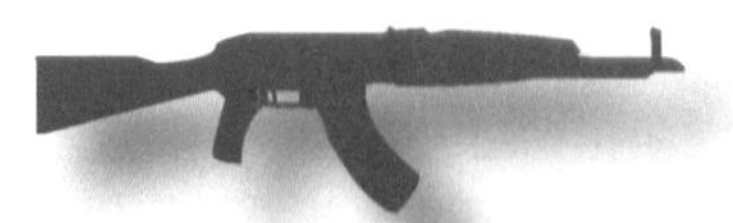

Chapter Twenty-Three

Rico and his girlfriend Angel decided they would enjoy this little vacation by first wandering around the square and them Walmart before deciding which restaurant to try for dinner. Walking hand in hand, around the square, Angel stopped outside to shop named "Surprise". Let's go in! They have some really cute things!"

The bell jangled over the door as they entered. Roz called out, "Welcome! Let me know if I can help." "We're just looking!" Rico answered. "Look away," Roz replied. Roz had to take a deep breath when she realized who had walked in. She worked on ignoring them as she restacked the tee shirts she had just stacked. Angel selected a sun catcher shaped like a starfish and looked pleadingly at Rico. "Would you buy this for me please?" It is very reasonable, and I can remember our little vacation." "Sure," Rico replied taking pride in his ability to buy her something. He swaggered up to the cash register and called out, "We'd like tp buy this!" "Certainly." Roz answered. "Oh, I just love those sun catchers. Are y'all visiting?" "Just passing through, Rico replied. "Will this be cash or charge?" "Cash, it will be cash." Roz finished the sale, bagged the starfish and carefully slipped the bills into the drawers as untouched as possible. As they left, she called out, "Come again".

Roz gave them time to clear the area, watching as they wandered down the street to the café. She called Mark and told him she had made contact with the young couple and had the money he used to pay if he wanted to try to retrieve fingerprints. "Thanks Roz, I'll be right there and coming in you back door." Mark arrived five minutes later putting the bills in an evidence bag. "Thanks, Roz. This is a long shot, but I will be good to know who he is?"

Rico and Angel had dinner at the local Mexican restaurant as a finale to their weekend. As they walked slowly back to Motel 8, neither noticed the man in the shadows watching. Dad had said to get back to Mobile so they prepared to leave early the next morning.

There was a discussion in State Police Headquarters whether to hold them, but they put a tracker on the car and notified the Alabama officials of the cocaine connection. The minute Rico's car crossed the state line; the appropriate officers would know and keep tabs on their car.

Their uneventful arrival back in Mobile was noted. Dad immediately sat Rico down to interrogate. "What did you do? What did you hear exactly?" When they related the conversation, his Dad sat a moment. "I think," he said "one more run will be it. If Mafia is there, we have covered ourselves well so shouldn't be a problem. One more Saturday and we move on to a new area. The fudge has been a clever disguise but the fudge shops are far apart. One more trip there we move on. We'll be good and gone by next Saturday night. His words were prophesy as the next Saturday was indeed their last

Laverne and Floyd Jones meanwhile had broken camp and were traveling North through town. Laverne sighed and commented. These small town are really boring. Nothing ever really happens in them.!" "Hmmm" Lloyd mused. "I wouldn't' t be too sure about that."

The state papers were full of the big bust a week later when the entire Mobile ring was arrested. Young Rico the lowest in the gang got the least sentence. The court showed mercy to Consuela and Savannah Sue assured her a job so she could bring her children to live with her.

The mafia had a celebration dinner together to rehash the excitement of the trial and were secretly awarded a citation by the state police for their part in the apprehension and ultimate incarceration of a very large drug cartel from Alabama to Kansas City and beyond. The girls settled down for the mundane events of a small town life. That is until they stumble on another adventure.

The End (or is it?)

9 7 9 8 8 9 3 9 1 7 3 3 8